This book belongs to

_____

The Owl and the Pussycat

By Edward Lear

Illustrated by Nancy Sippel Carpenter

DERRYDALE BOOKS
New York / Avenel, New Jersey

The Owl and the Pussy-Cat went to sea
In a beautiful pea-green boat.
They took some honey, and plenty of money
Wrapped up in a five-pound note.

The Owl looked up to the stars above,
And sang to a small guitar,
"O lovely Pussy, O Pussy, my love,
What a beautiful Pussy you are,
    You are,
    You are!
What a beautiful Pussy you are!"

Pussy said to the Owl, "You elegant fowl,
    How charmingly sweet you sing!
Oh! let us be married; too long we have tarried:
    But what shall we do for a ring?"

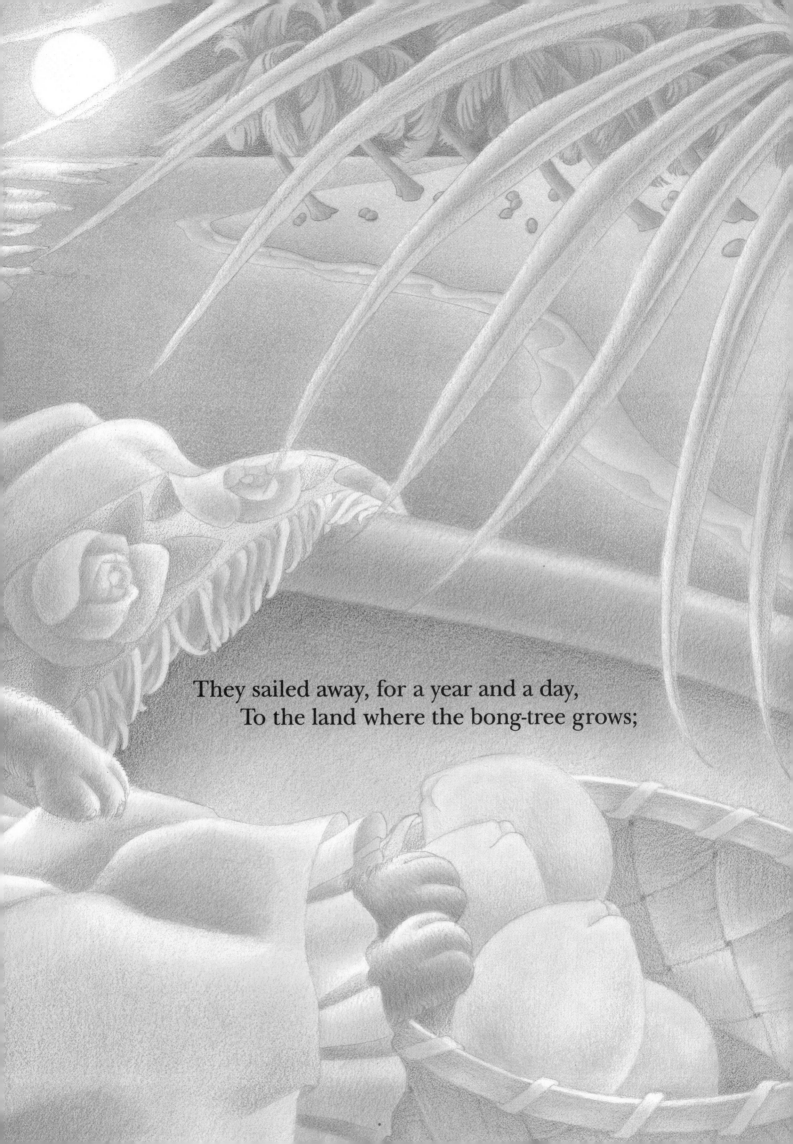

They sailed away, for a year and a day,
To the land where the bong-tree grows;

And there in a wood a Piggy-wig stood,
With a ring at the end of his nose,
His nose,
His nose,
With a ring at the end of his nose.

"Dear Pig, are you willing to sell for one shilling
Your ring?" Said the Piggy, "I will."
So they took it away, and were married next day
By the Turkey who lives on the hill.

They dined on mince and slices of quince,
Which they ate with a runcible spoon;

And hand in hand, on the edge of the sand
They danced by the light of the moon,
The moon,
The moon,
They danced by the light of the moon.